DATE DUE

AUG. 4 1993			

F
Bun
Bunting, Eve
The Mask

ENCYCLOPAEDIA BRITANNICA
EDUCATIONAL CORPORATION
310 S. Michigan Avenue • Chicago, Illinois 60604

85660

THE
MASK

Text copyright 1992 by The Child's World, Inc.
All rights reserved. No part of this book may be
reproduced or utilized in any form or by any means
without written permission from the Publisher.
Printed in the United States of America.

Designed by Bill Foster of Albarella & Associates, Inc.

Distributed to schools and libraries
in the United States by
ENCYCLOPAEDIA BRITANNICA EDUCATIONAL CORP
310 South Michigan Ave.
Chicago, Illinois 60604

Library of Congress Cataloging-in-Publication Data
Bunting, Eve, 1928-
The mask/Eve Bunting.
p.   cm.
Summary: When Matt's father purchases an old Chinese
mask, strange things begin to happen inside Matthew's
head.
ISBN 0-89565-769-4
[1. Extrasensory perception – Fiction.]   I. Title.
PZ7.B91527Mas   1991
[Fic]—dc20   91-17319
                                               CIP
                                               AC

69633

THE MASK

Eve Bunting

Illustrated by

Duane Krych

THE CHILD'S WORLD

My name is Matthew McShane. I'm thirteen years old and there's something very creepy about me. I've known about the creepy thing for a long time, since I was about eight or nine, but I don't talk about it. I sort of did, way back at the beginning, but I could tell people didn't believe me, so I quit. Mr. Bramley, who's the visiting psychologist at school suspects, I think, and he tried to get me to spill everything, but I clammed up. Who wants to be different? Who wants to be a freak? I think maybe my friend Clinker knows, but he doesn't want to hear about it. I guess it scares him. It sure scares me. Mr. Bramley says E.S.P. is a gift…a bonus in life. Mr. Bramley doesn't know what he's talking about.

Thank goodness my E.S.P. or whatever doesn't happen too often. But it's happening now, and it looks like it's not going away.

It has to do with the new door knocker Dad just put on our front door. We got the knocker in a little Chinese store in Hawaii when we were there on vacation a week or so ago. The second I saw it, my tingling started. Did you ever wear a wool sweater right next to your skin and feel every little hair on your arms and body stick up like a barb and attach itself to that scrubby old wool? Even hair on your back and chest that isn't even there yet? Well, that's the way the tingling is. And man, did that door knocker make me tingle!

Dad spotted it in a box that had been pushed under a back counter. He fished it out and dusted it off.

Mom sighed.

Dad is what he calls "a collector" and what Mom calls a "junk gatherer." He loves to make finds. We have more swords and gurka knives and warrior spears hanging on the walls of our den than you'd ever find in the

National Gallery.

Dad held the door knocker at arm's length. It was bronze and shaped like a round face with holes for eyes. A curved piece of metal drooped like a mustache. I guess that was the knocking part.

"Ugh," Mom said.

"Fantastic," Dad murmured.

I just stood there in my new Hawaiian shirt, tingling myself to death.

The store was called the Yin and Yang. It was probably Mr. Yin who came over to smile up at Dad.

"Interesting art object," Mr. Yin said. "It is old door guardian. Often made in shape of dragon's head."

Dad poked a finger in one of the empty eye sockets. "It looks more like a human face than a dragon's head," he said. "Could it be a mask of some sort?"

I could tell that Mr. Yin knew a collector when he saw one. "Could be yes," he said.

"Person make clay mask." He demonstrated spreading clay over his cheeks. "Later, cast in bronze."

"Um." Dad turned the knocker over and over.

"Probably early Chou period." Mr. Yin said.

I was tingling so bad that I picked up one of Mr. Yin's back scratchers and worked it up under the back of my shirt when no one was looking.

Scratch, scratch, scratch.

"I let you have it for eighty dollars,"

Mr. Yin said.

"Oh, Harold!" Mom had her "please don't buy any more junk" voice, but as usual the sight of an "objet d'art" had turned Dad totally deaf.

"We'll take it," he said.

Mom signed over the last of our traveler's checks and Dad put the wrapped-up door knocker into the carrier bag we'd bought.

"You carry it, Matthew," he said, putting the bag between my feet.

I stared down at it. I didn't want to carry it. In the first place, the tingling had stopped now that the mask was out of sight. In the second place, nobody with any self respect would want to carry the dumb-looking bag with its dumb-looking picture of hula dancers in their dumb grass skirts.

"I'm pooped," I whined. But no-body paid any attention so I grabbed the bag. Did you ever grab an electric vibrator?

"I'm pooped too," Mom said. "There's something about using up the last traveler's check that'll do it to you."

Dad slapped Mom on the back. "It's bad luck to take money home from a vacation." he said. "And this time tomorrow we'll be back in California."

Sitting on the plane the next day I began to wonder if maybe I'd imagined the whole thing. I mean the tingling. It could have been sunburn, couldn't it? That's the funny thing about my affliction. I can usually convince myself afterwards that there's some kind of normal explanation. Like now. Dad had put the mask into his suitcase and it had disappeared somewhere with the rest of the luggage into the belly of the airplane. And I was feeling OK again. I nibbled at my nails, thinking back to other tingling times. Like the day we were all sitting outside in our back yard under the sycamore tree. And I knew the big branch was going to break and fall before it did. I just started to tingle, and I looked up, and I knew.

"Run, run," I yelled.

I grabbed the chair Mom was sitting in and knocked her clean out of it, rolling her on the ground.

Dad had leaped up and the branch missed him by inches. The thing was as big as a telephone pole and would have squashed us to a pulp.

"But how did you know, Matthew?" Mom asked shakily, afterwards.

The tingling, I thought. And seeing it happen before it did. Seeing that big ugly branch break and come thudding down through the space and the silence.

"I think I heard it crack," I muttered.

And maybe that was all it had been, I thought now, biting away at my nails and looking at the Pacific Ocean way, way down below. And this time I was probably sunburned.

I had myself pretty well convinced until we got in our house and Dad dug out the mask.

We were in his and Mom's bedroom, surrounded by all our vacation loot.

"What do you think of it, Matthew?" Dad held up the bronze face.

I took a step backward and put my hands behind my back. Don't ask me to touch it, I thought. Just don't ask me to touch it.

"It's pretty…unique," I said. That's Dad's favorite word about his art objects. The blank mask eyes seemed to watch me as I tried to edge away.

"Are you going to put it on the den wall? Or on the door?" I was twitching, like a dog with fleas.

"The door."

"Oh. Well, I got to go, Dad. Clinker's waiting for me to go surfing."

As soon as I was outside, the tingling stopped. Well, I thought, at least he's keeping it out of the house. With it out

16

and me in, maybe it'll be OK.

I got my wet suit and my board and padded along the beach alley to Clinker's apartment. There was a nip of fall in the air and I could hear the whisper of the sea on the other side of the buildings that lined the beach. Colder than Hawaii, and the water would be colder too, though it was the same ocean. But if I couldn't live on Maui, California was for sure the next best thing.

I tried not to think about the mask, but it was hard. Always, before, the tingling had meant something. What did it mean this time? It would have been nice to tell Clinker about it, but he'd think I was bonkers and who would blame him?

Instead I told him how the waves had been on North Shore and described the way the surfers had to go beyond the reef at Waikiki.

We stayed till the evening glass-off and by the time I got back home I saw that Dad had the mask up on the front door. The sun turned the bronze to gold. But the creepiest thing was the way the eyes were. Our door is painted red and the eyes of the mask looked red too. Of course, I knew it was only the paint shining through the empty sockets, but it was super scary. The small colored glass panes that are set high on the door reflected beams of green and blue and yellow on the bronze, accenting it, as though picking it out in strobe lights. I shivered, feeling the clamminess of the wet suit, cold as seaweed against my skin and the tingling sparked up and down my arms and legs. I walked quickly round the back way, which is what I always do anyway.

The tingling stopped when I was inside. See, I thought. It can't get at me in here. I'll just keep well away from it. No sweat.

"That's the ugliest looking door knocker I've ever seen," Mom said at dinner. "I swear, it's like having a head skewered onto our front door."

I pushed my salad round and round on my plate and I tried not to think about whose face that had been. Was the mask made after he was dead, while he lay all cold and still?

"And it's so big," Mom went on. "That nice brass eagle looked just right on the door."

"That eagle was not unique," Dad said. "Sam stays where he is." He grinned at me. "I christened him. That's his name."

"Mu-lien," I said.

"What?" They were both staring at me.

The word hung on my tongue. "Mu-lien," I said again, as astonished as they were.

"Where did you get that from?"

I swallowed. "Oh...I...He looks more Chinese than Sam," I said weakly.

The wind came up later and we could hear the rush and pound of the ocean against the rocks. We were watching TV in the den when I heard the knocking at the front door. It was a hollow, metallic sort of knock. My nonexistent chest hairs pricked up their ears. I looked at Dad. He was sitting back in his chair.

Knock, knock, knock.

I bristled.

Mom yawned and picked up the TV guide.

"There's…there's someone at the door," I said. My mouth was numb.

"I didn't hear the bell," Mom said.

"It's…they knocked."

"Well, go see who it is, Matthew," Dad told me.

I didn't want to go to the door. No way did I want to go to the door. But what could I do? Or say?

I clicked on the porch light in the hallway so that the front of the house and yard were shadowless. Then I peered through the colored glass. Whichever pane you look through sets the color of the outside world and I saw it, a deep, rich, empty green. No one there.

If I squinted down I could just see the top of the mask, the curve of the top of the head. And something else. The brass, metal ring that was the clapper, or whatever you call the part on the knocker that knocks. It was raised, standing straight out all by itself, ready to fall and make that clatter again. And there was no one there. I stepped back just as the knocker fell smash against the metal.

Then I was running, careening along the hallway, back to the safety of the den.

Dad raised his eyebrows at me. "What's the rush?"

I stood, trying to get my heart out of my throat and back to my chest where it belonged.

"Was someone there, dear?" Mom asked.

"No," I said.

Knock, knock, knock.

I picked up the *Sports Illustrated* and hid behind it.

Knock, knock, knock.

Was I the only one who could hear it?

"Do you usually read with the magazine upside down, Matt?" Mom asked me mildly.

"Is that someone at the door again?" I cocked my head to one side.

"I don't hear anything."

"Oh."

I stayed up real late. I even watched The Late Show with them. And I hate

The Late Show. But I wasn't about to go along that hallway by myself and up those lonely stairs.

It wasn't so bad when I was in bed because my room is at the back and if there was more knocking I couldn't hear it. I fell asleep at last to the sound of the surf that has been part of my life for as long as I can remember.

I wakened once and the wind had died. I listened, and I could hear nothing. Nervously I got out of bed and tiptoed to the top of the stairs. Silence hung heavy around me. Below, I could see the strips of red and blue and green moonlight lying in bars across the tiles of the hallway floor. No sound at all. But I didn't go down there. It always bugs me when

26

kids in movies and books do dumb things like walking alone at night into the haunted house and stuff like that. No way. I got back into my safe, warm bed and lay there, thinking. Sure! When the wind stopped, the sound stopped. That clapper was probably real light and the wind was able to lift it and drop it again. Why hadn't I thought of that? And Mom and Dad hadn't heard it because, well, because people don't hear as well at forty as they do at thirteen. It made sense. I felt better about the whole thing. Until I remembered Mu-lien. Then I was awake again. But after a while I was able to rationalize that too. I'd probably seen an old Chinese painting somewhere and the name had stuck in my subconscious. Mr. Bramley says people have more memories floating around in their heads than there are fish in the ocean, and that's probably the one true thing Mr. Bramley did say. I felt so good that I dropped off to sleep right away.

*T*hings were OK for about three days. There was no wind and no knocking and I guess I was, what you might call, lulled into a false sense of security. So I wasn't feeling too bad about being alone in the house at night. Until the knocking started.

Mom had left dinner for me, and I'd just finished it and was settling down with the new September *Surfing*. Clinker had called to say there were some great shots of Jerry Lopez riding the big Makaha swells in the centerfold. I'd just opened to the color pictures when the knocking started.

I froze.

Knock, knock, knock.

The magazine rattled and shook in my hands like a train on a track.

Then I heard something else. The wind had risen and changed direction. We could always tell by the different sounds of the sea. Now I could hear the waves crashing and booming against the rocks and around the pilings.

Knock, knock, knock.

Sure! It was the wind doing it again.

I studied Jerry Lopez. He was riding the tube, water curling around him in a translucent pipe, green as Mom's jade ring.

Knock, knock, knock.

Only the wind. My hand's were sweating. I thought of the front door, the mask nailed to it, the red eyes staring, the clapper moving up and down.

I could tape the clapper down. I could get that heavy brown wrapping tape and stick it over the mustache, and over the mouth…

Knock, knock, knock.

I jumped up. I couldn't touch it. I couldn't put my hands near it. But I could go look. I could see how strong the wind was. Or was that too much like the dumb storybook kids who were always going out at night into the graveyard to search for the vampire? Naw! The door was locked. The chain would be on it. What could happen?

I cat-footed down the hallway, hugging the wall, holding my breath. My fingernails scratched at the tingling that had begun on the side of my neck.

I put my face against the colored panes.

Every tree in the yard swayed and danced and rattled. The grass that I was supposed to cut yesterday and didn't, fluttered and rippled. See? See the wind?

I brought my eyes down to the edge of the porch and heard my heart begin to thud. Mom's ferns in their hanging baskets hung still and quiet and I realized that the wind was blowing across the porch, not getting inside it at all. The broad leaves of the potted rubber tree stood motionless.

Knock, knock, knock.

This time it was so loud that I almost jumped right out of my tingling skin.

Then a voice. Right there, right here. Outside the door? Inside my head?

"Let me go!"

I backed away. Terror was bubbling in me, spilling from me.

Knock, Knock, Knock.

I ran up the stairs, leaping, stumbling, taking them three at a time.

I got in my parents' room and locked the door and leaned against it. I wanted to pull all the furniture over and pile it, like a barricade. I wanted to hide under the bed.

The phone was on the bedside table and I knew where they were. It took my fingers three tries before they pushed the right buttons. I asked Mrs. Lang for Mom and while I waited I watched my white face and buggy eyes looking back at me from the mirror over her dresser.

"I'm sick," I told her when she came on the line. "I'm really sick. Can you come home? Please?"

"Is that Matthew?" she asked in a

puzzled sort of way, and I realized that I was talking so funny she hadn't even recognized her own son.

They were back in less than fifteen minutes and I guarantee they were the longest fifteen minutes of my whole life.

I was still locked in their room and I didn't even want to open the door for them.

Dad sat down beside me on the bed and I told them straight off what had happened. The knocking and the voice and everything. So what if they thought their only son was a freak? Or bonkers. I didn't care anymore.

I glanced up at once and saw them looking at each other in a dazed sort of way.

Mom went to get the thermometer which began to make me mad. That wasn't the kind of sick I was. But I guess I couldn't blame her. Not really.

Dad tightened his arm around my shoulders. "We'll take the mask off tomorrow and get rid of it," he said. "Tonight even. Right now. You're not to worry anymore about it."

I nodded, clenching my teeth to keep them from clicking. I wanted to tell him that was pretty nice of him. He's always very attached to his "objets d'art." But I didn't trust my voice.

Mom tucked me up in my own bed and brought me a cup of hot milk. I hate hot milk. But it does warm you up when your flesh is shivering.

Dad came in my room. He had his big pipewrench in his hand.

"Right now, Matthew," he said quietly.

"You won't bring it in the house, will you?" My voice climbed the walls and hung somewhere near the ceiling.

"I won't bring it in the house."

"OK." I turned my face to the wall and listened to him go downstairs. I heard the door open and pulled the covers up tight over my head.

He was taking a long time to get it off. An awfully long time.

I lay, listening, straining to hear. At last I got out of bed and went to the top of the stairs.

Cold air drifted up from below so I knew the front door was open. I crouched down and held on to the stair rail.

"Dad?"

His voice floated up to me. "I can't get the darn thing off, Matthew. It's…"

Mom came running up the stairs. She must have been helping him. I couldn't get over how brave they both were. "He put it on with bolts, honey. And he tightened them up real good and they won't come loose."

"You mean, it has to stay there?" Squeaky voice again, rising up the walls to hang, like vapor, over my head.

"He's putting some loosening oil on it, Matt," Mom soothed. "It'll come off."

But it didn't.

"Darndest thing," Dad said after he'd worked on it for about an hour. "I'll leave the oil on all night. It's as if the bolts are rusted. But how could they be? That door knocker's only been on, what? Three or four days?" He wiped his hands on a rag. "I'll buy a hacksaw in the morning and I'll cut it off if I have to. Soon as the stores open tomorrow, Matt. I promise."

"Sure," I said.

We all stood, looking at each other.

"You know what?" Mom said. "Why don't you get your sleeping bag, hon, and bunk down in our room tonight? I mean, heck, there's no sense risking any more bad dreams."

That's what they thought it had been. They thought I'd fallen asleep on the couch and dreamt the whole thing. For a minute I was mad again, the way I'd been when Mom went for the thermometer. But I knew I had no right to be mad. They were being super nice about it anyway. Not many parents would spend all this time getting rid of something just because a kid had bad dreams.

"Thanks," I said. "It's a good idea about the sleeping bag."

Neither of them seemed to notice that I squeezed my sleeping bag into the small space between their bed and the wall, well away from the bedroom door.

My sleeping bag is down, goose down, and it's the most comfortable place in the whole world. The tightness of it is secure, somehow protective. When I listened, all I could hear was the good, reassuring sound of my parents' breathing and the low whisper of the ocean. If I stretched out my hand I could touch their bed covers. I felt really safe, and I began to wonder myself if I had dropped off to sleep on the couch. That's almost the worst thing about my affliction. The way you begin to doubt yourself when everything's normal again.

The warm milk and the warm sleeping bag began to do their thing. I heard Mom whisper, "Matthew? Are you asleep?" and I was so close to it that I didn't try to answer her.

*T*his time I was dreaming.

In my dream I wakened and sat up and slipped out of my sleeping bag. Someone was calling, and I had to go.

I tiptoed past the bed where my parents slept and I opened the door and slithered downstairs. I walked through the bars of color on the hall floor. In my dream I felt the coldness of the tiles, and the coldness was as real as if I were awake. But I couldn't be, because I'd never be doing this if I were awake. In the house around me nothing moved. There was no sound. I opened the front door and stood, face to face with the mask.

I stretched out my hand and took hold of the ring that hung from the bronzed, carved lips, and it was like gripping a live electric wire. Current shot up my arm and I knew then that I was awake, not dreaming, because no one could have slept through a jolt like that. I was here, doing this, me, alone, and I knew it, and I tried to drop the curve of wire, but it stuck to my hand, welded to it, and then, and then…

Everything had changed.

There was a sea, but it was not my sea. And there was a time, but it was not my time.

I was watching a play that I had no part in.

The ocean hammered against the rocks, spouting up in crests and spumes of spray. People stood on a low jetty. People from a long time past. The wind billowed their long robes around them and plucked at their tall, jewelled headdresses. It was almost dusk, with a dark sea and sky, and there was one figure, center stage, that drew my eyes and held them.

It was a girl, a beautiful girl in a white dress, so filmy that it swirled around her like a gossamer cloud.

Two men held her, one on either side, and she was struggling. Words came to me, a buzz of strange words that meant nothing to me.

Behind the girl was another struggling figure. This time it was a young man in a sea-green robe. He was fighting to get to her, but the men held him back.

Then, for the first time, I noticed the flat, barge-like boat that bobbed in the swells at the end of the jetty.

The girl suddenly broke free and turned, holding out her arms toward the man who struggled behind her.

"Mu-lien," she screamed. The word was high and pitiful as a seagull's cry and it was torn from her lips and tossed by the wind across the dark sea.

The green-robed man yelled three words. I knew what they were even though I'd never heard them before in my life.

"Let me go!" he begged. "Let me go!"

He hurled himself against the bodies that surrounded him and for a heartbeat I thought he would get free, fight through to her, save her from whatever was going to happen.

But a hand raised a rock, and the man's body slumped forward, held upright only by his captors.

The girl's head drooped and her own struggling ceased.

Six men raised her high and placed her on the flat deck of the barge.

She lay, facing the sky with her

eyes closed and her hands folded across her breast. The white cloud of her robe moved gently in the night air.

Someone loosened the mooring rope and the barge drifted free. There must have been tides here, or currents that were strong as the ones by our jetty. Slowly the barge moved out and away.

As the shadows closed around it the chanting began, low and sad and melancholy. When the sea was empty, the singing ceased. With heads lowered the robed figures filed away and I saw that Mu-lien was being carried between two bearers. I saw the green robe trailing in the rocks and sand.

On the misty surface of the sea there was only a dark glint of moonlight and one faint cry, like that of a lonely gull.

I stood very still. I was colder than I had ever been and when I looked down I saw that there was something in my hand. I stared down at it. It was a metal ring, and I wasn't anywhere, watching a play, I was here. This was the front porch of my own house, and that was the sound of my own sea that I was hearing. I was standing with my hand on the mask of Mu-lien.

It was very odd. The fear inside me had all gone. And there was no tingling. It was as if a message had been sent and received and now an unseen hand had turned off the current.

I looked at the mask. Had the blow on his head killed him then? Had he died, even as she cried to him? Had someone, for some reason of his own, made this mask so that something of Mu-lien would remain when all else had crumbled?

"Let me go!" Those were the words he'd cried then. And thousands of years later he was crying the same words.

I tried the bolts. They were loose and turned eagerly in my fingers. The oil? I wondered. Or something else?

I had the mask in my hands. The empty eyes seemed to look beyond me and the mouth smiled a half-smile.

I walked across our yard and along the alley. There was an opening here that gave public access to the beach and I moved like a shadow between the tall, sleeping apartments. Somewhere, on a top floor, a light gleamed yellow through the darkness.

I walked on the water's edge where the sea foam clotted around my feet, where the sea licked around the bottoms of my pajamas.

The ocean sound was louder here, by the jetty.

I climbed up over the rocks, holding the mask cradled against my chest.

I'd thought it was the wind that caused the frantic rapping I'd heard. But of course, it hadn't been. The wind had brought with it the sound of the sea, and the sound of the sea had carried its own memories.

Part way along the jetty I found the bottom of an old tomato crate that

52

had come in with the tide and had stayed, stranded. I carried it with me, and when I got to the place where the jetty ended I knelt and floated the wood on the water. Then I placed the mask on it and pushed the small raft out where the tide could catch it.

The sightless eyes stared up at the Pacific sky and I stood there, watching until all I could see was darkness. For a second, I was sure I could hear the far-away, long-lost sound of chanting but it might have been only the rising of the wind.

Then, as I turned away, I thought I heard something else. The cry of gulls, joyous and happy, clamoring together in the silence of the night.

But maybe I only imagined it. All of

it. That's almost the worst thing about my affliction. The way you begin to doubt yourself when everything's normal again.